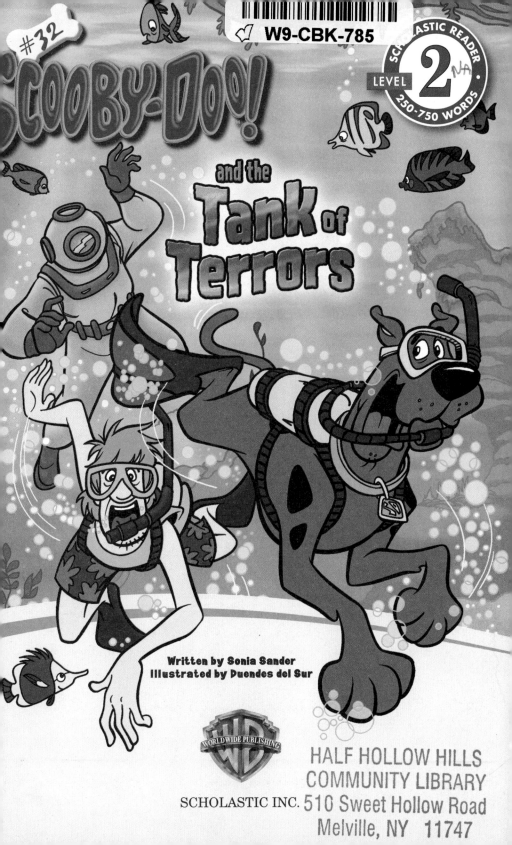

#32

SCOOBY-DOO!
and the
Tank of
Terrors

SCHOLASTIC READER
LEVEL 2
250-750 WORDS

W9-CBK-785

Written by Sonia Sander
Illustrated by Duendes del Sur

WORLDWIDE PUBLISHING

SCHOLASTIC INC.

ISBN 978-0-545-40318-4

12 11 10 9 8 7 6 5 4 3 2 1   12 13 14 15 16 17/0

Designed by Henry Ng

Printed in the U.S.A.   40

First printing, September 2012

Scooby-Doo and the kids from Mystery, Inc. were on their way to the aquarium. They were going to help with the sea animals.

"Come on, gang," called Fred. "We're late for our tour. Let's go inside the aquarium."

"Thanks for coming today," said the manager, Mike Manatee. "The tanks need a good clean."

"Yeah, everyone has been too afraid of the ghost diver to go inside," added Barry Barracuda, Mike's assistant.

"*G-g-g-host?*" gasped Shaggy. "Like, did you say ghost diver?"

"That's just an old legend," said Mike. "Some folks say he's searching for his long-lost buried treasure. But don't worry . . . it's not true."

"*Ree-hee-hee-hee-hee,*" Scooby-Doo giggled. The octopus was tickling him!

"Like, Barry Barracuda could have told us about the kooky octopus!" said Shaggy.

"I think it's sweet, Shaggy," said Daphne. "She just wants to play with you."

"Like, a silly octopus beats a spooky ghost any day," said Shaggy.

"Shaggy!" cried Velma. "That food is for the skates."

"Like, we were just making sure it was okay for the skates to eat," said Shaggy.

"Jeepers!" called Daphne. "Look what I found! A gold coin!"

Barry grabbed the coin. "Must be a fake some kid threw into the tank," he said. "I'll bring it to the lost and found."

That's when the gang got another surprise.
"Zoinks! The ghost diver!" cried Shaggy.
"Like, let's make some waves!"
Scooby and the gang swam across the tank as fast as they could.

Fred spied a cave. The gang slipped inside and waited till the diver disappeared again.

"Jeepers," said Daphne. "That was close. But why is there a cave in the aquarium?"

"It's a storage closet," said Fred. "Look! There's a vacuum in here."

"That isn't a vacuum," said Velma. "It's a metal detector."

Before the gang could find out more, something found them!

"*Ree-hee-hee-hee-hee*," Scooby-Doo giggled. Only it wasn't the octopus tickling him, it was the ghost diver!

"Like, that spooky snorkeler is back!" cried Shaggy.

The gang was on the run again. With the ghost diver closing in, they needed a hiding place — fast!

"Look!" cried Daphne. "Let's go into the old mini-sub ride!"

"Jinkies!" said Velma. "Look at these maps of the tanks. Someone has been busy searching for something."

"I bet I know who," added Fred.

"I know what the ghost diver is looking for," said Daphne, holding up another gold coin.

"Wait a minute," said Velma. "I've seen that coin before. A few years ago, someone stole a hundred coins like that from the aquarium's buried treasure display. No one ever found the coins or the thief."

Daphne nodded. "The thief must have hidden the coins in another part of the aquarium — like the tank."

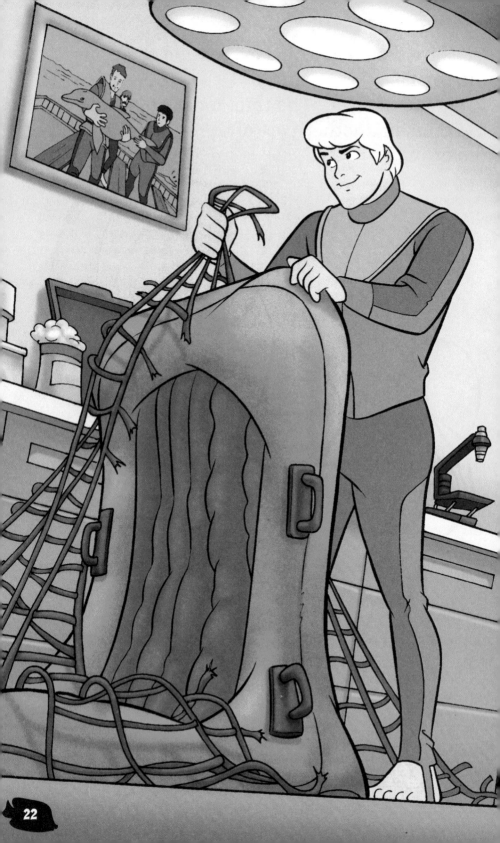

"Okay, gang," said Fred. "It's time to set a trap and catch this creepy ghost crook. I know just how to do it."

"Like, please don't say me and Scoob are the bait," said Shaggy.

But Fred's plan was already in place.
He'd set up a big net in one of the
tanks. As usual, Scooby and Shaggy
were the bait.

"Roh rell," sighed Scooby.

"Like, it would be nice if we could choose our part in the plan just once," moaned Shaggy.

Fred, Daphne, and Velma waited for the ghost diver to come after Scooby and Shaggy. Then they turned on the tank's whirlpool. The water jets pushed the net right into the ghost diver! Soon he was all tangled up.

The gang pulled the ghost diver out of the tank.

"I think it's about time we find out who's hiding under this helmet!" said Fred.

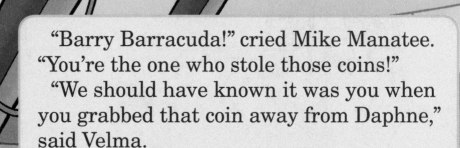

"Barry Barracuda!" cried Mike Manatee. "You're the one who stole those coins!"

"We should have known it was you when you grabbed that coin away from Daphne," said Velma.

"I'd be rich if it weren't for you meddling kids!" cried Barry.

THE
SCOOBY-DOO!
AQUATIC SHOW

As a thank you, Mike Manatee made Scooby and Shaggy the stars of the sea lion show.

"*Scooby-Dooby-Doo!*" shouted Scooby.